The author knew
(as authors do)
that each of her readers was special.
This one is for you.
—K. D.

For Carol
—C. R.

atheneum

ATHENEUM BOOKS FOR YOUNG READERS
An imprint of Simon & Schuster Children's Publishing Division
1230 Avenue of the Americas, New York, New York 10020
Text copyright © 2017 by Kelly DiPuccio
Illustrations copyright © 2017 by Christian Robinson
ATHENEUM BOOKS FOR YOUNG READERS is a registered trademark of Simon & Schuster, Inc.
Atheneum logo is a trademark of Simon & Schuster, Inc.
For information about special discounts for bulk purchases, please contact Simon & Schuster Special Sales at 1-866-506-1949 or business@simonandschuster.com.
The Simon & Schuster Speakers Bureau can bring authors to your live event. For more information or to book an event, contact the Simon & Schuster Speakers Bureau at 1-866-248-3049 or visit our website at www.simonspeakers.com.
Book design by Ann Bobco
The text for this book was set in Adobe Caslon Pro.
The illustrations for this book were rendered in acrylic paint.
Manufactured in China
1216 SCP
First Edition
10 9 8 7 6 5 4 3 2 1
Library of Congress Cataloging-in-Publication Data
Names: DiPuccio, Kelly, author. | Robinson, Christian, illustrator.
Title: Antoinette / words by Kelly DiPuccio ; pictures by Christian Robinson.
Description: First edition. | New York : Atheneum Books for Young Readers, [2017] | Summary: "Raised in a family of talented bulldogs, Antoinette the poodle wonders what makes her special. She gets the chance to prove herself and find what she's good at when puppy Ooh-La-La goes missing"—Provided by publisher.
Identifiers: LCCN 2015024845| ISBN 9781481457835 (hardcover) | ISBN 9781481457842 (eBook)
Subjects: | CYAC: Poodles—Fiction. | Bulldog—Fiction. | Dogs—Fiction. | Ability—Fiction.
Classification: LCC PZ7.D6219 An 2017 | DDC [E]—dc23
LC record available at http://lccn.loc.gov/2015024845

Antoinette

WORDS BY
KELLY DiPUCCHIO

PICTURES BY
CHRISTIAN ROBINSON

 Atheneum Books for Young Readers   New York · London · Toronto · Sydney · New Delhi

Mrs. Bulldog
watched
her puppies
race through
the yard.

ROCKY,

RICKY,

BRUNO,

and
ANTOINETTE.

RICKY,

BRUNO,

and
ANTOINETTE.

Busy, aren't they? And ridiculously cute,
but please don't tell them that.

PHOOEY!

Mrs. Bulldog knew (as mothers do)
that each of her puppies was special.

RICKY was *fast*!

"Superb."

ROCKY was clever.

"Outstanding."

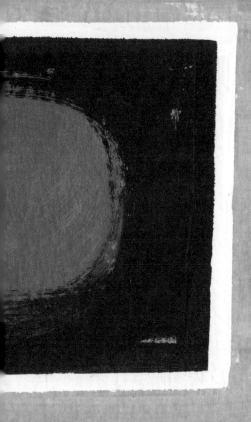

And
ANTOINETTE?

BRUNO
was
STRONG.

"Impressive."

Well, unlike
her burly brothers,
she still hadn't quite
discovered what
she was good at.

"Chin up!"
barked her mother.
"You
have something
extra special.
I can feel it
in my bones!"

ANTOINETTE was not so sure.

Every day the family went to the park
to play with their doggy friends.

Fi-Fi,

Foo-Foo, Ooh-La-La,

and

Gaston.

ANTOINETTE was fond of
Fi-Fi, Foo-Foo, Ooh-La-La . . .
and especially Gaston.

There was much
to chase after
in the park.
Biscuits. Balls. Butterflies.

Oh, boy.
There
seems
to be a
problem.

YIP! YIP! YIP!

"A puppy is missing!"
Mrs. Bulldog announced.

The pups
gathered
around.

ROCKY, RICKY, BRUNO, and **ANTOINETTE,**
followed by *Fi-Fi, Foo-Foo* . . . and *Gaston*.

"*Where is* **Ooh-La-La**?!"
Mrs. Poodle asked frantically.

Mrs. Bulldog comforted her friend. "We will find her!" she insisted.

ROCKY was clever, and he tracked paw prints in the mud.
No ***Ooh-La-La***.

RICKY was fast, and he raced around the lake in no time at all.

No ***Ooh-La-La***.

BRUNO was strong, and he left no stone unturned.
Still. No **Ooh-La-La**.

Mrs. Poodle cried out in desperation,

*"Whatever
shall
we do?"*

In that moment
ANTOINETTE
felt a tug in her heart and
a twitch in her nose.
She could not—
would not—
give up!

ANTOINETTE sniffed sidewalks.

And street vendors.

And sign posts.

The fearless pup dodged buggies and bicycles and broomsticks.

Not even a loud,

hungry garbage truck could slow her down.

When the parade of dogs
approached the entrance
to the city's museum,
ANTOINETTE
began to yap loudly.

YAP!
YAP!
YAP!

"NO DOGS ALLOWED!"
the guard said gruffly, pointing to the sign.

But **ANTOINETTE** was unstoppable!
She ran circles around the guard,
dashed through the doors,
and raced down a long corridor.

ANTOINETTE burst through the crowd just in time . . .

YAP! YAP! YAP!

to save **Ooh-La-La** from a perilous fall.

Would you like to see that again?

Well done,
ANTOINETTE.

"*Merci! Merci!*"
Mrs. Poodle said,
panting happily.
"You found my
Ooh-La-La!"

Mrs. Bulldog
was beaming with pride.
"You were remarkably brave,"
she said to her daughter
with a wink.

ANTOINETTE
smiled.

Gaston
smiled too.

And many years later,

while **ANTOINETTE** and *Gaston* were raising a busy family of their own,

ANTOINETTE followed her heart (and her nose!)
and became one of the most famous
police dogs ever to patrol the streets of Paris.